A TROUBLING CASE OF MURDER ON THE MENU

AN EMILY CHERRY COZY MYSTERY
BOOK ONE

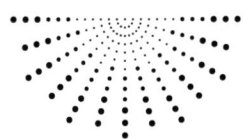

DONNA DOYLE

PUREREAD.COM

Copyright © 2023 PureRead Ltd

www.pureread.com

All rights reserved. No part of this publication may be reproduced, distributed or transmitted in any form or by any means, without prior written permission.

Publisher's Note: This is a work of fiction. Names, characters, places, and incidents are a product of the author's imagination. Locales and public names are sometimes used for atmospheric purposes. Any resemblance to actual people, living or dead, or to businesses, companies, events, institutions, or locales is completely coincidental.

CONTENTS

Chapter 1	1
Chapter 2	15
Chapter 3	29
Chapter 4	40
Chapter 5	55
Chapter 6	71
Chapter 7	85
Chapter 8	98
Chapter 9	115
Emily's Next Adventure…	129
Other Books In This Series	145
So much more to enjoy!	147
Our Gift To You	151

CHAPTER ONE

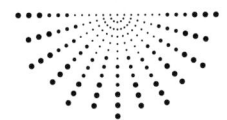

"These green beans are yucky!"

"They're not yucky, honey. And you really shouldn't say that. Gran made those."

Emily Cherry smiled across the table at her youngest grandchild. "It's all right, Ella. They did turn out rather yucky, didn't they?"

Phoebe looked across the table at her mother. "They're just a little under seasoned, Mum. Ella can put a little salt on them and she'll be just fine."

Hearing this, three-year-old Ella grabbed the saltshaker and dusted her green beans with a heavy blizzard of the stuff. Emily pressed her lips together to contain a laugh. She could see that Phoebe was rather distraught, and even though Emily was old enough to be retired after a full career, she very well remembered what it was like to raise little ones.

"Mom, have you looked over that information I left last time about the cruise?" Nathan, her oldest, had come straight from work and was still dressed in a dark suit. He was a handsome man, with sandy brown hair and dark blue eyes that reminded Emily so much of her late husband.

"I did, but I don't think it's anything I'll do at this time," Emily replied as she cut thoughtfully into her tenderloin. It seemed as though she was doing everything thoughtfully lately. The past year or so had been so strange, and her life had changed so much, that she felt as though she had to consider every move she made.

"You'd really love it," Nathan's wife Genevieve enthused. She'd hardly touched her dinner, but Emily didn't think that had anything to do with how it tasted. Genevieve was a glamorous woman who always had her hair styled and her makeup perfect, and she had a closet the size of most people's bedrooms, which was full of designer clothes.. She did some sort of work in the fashion industry, but Emily had never really quite understood what her job was. "Nathan and I went on a cruise a couple of years ago. It was so relaxing!"

"You know, I'm not sure I want to relax that much," Emily began.

"Yes, and you could take your knitting!" Mavis interrupted. She, too, was still dressed from work in a slim black skirt suit. It was a little severe for her thin frame, but she was always trying to make an impression at her tech firm. "Just think about it, Mom! You could sit out on the deck, knitting away and making all your Christmas presents early."

Emily shook her head. "I do more than knit, you know. Besides, that's a better task for when it's cold and nasty outside."

"I've heard of people taking books on holiday with them," Phoebe added quietly as she handed her daughter Lucy an extra napkin. "Not that I would know! We've talked and talked about taking a trip, but there's always something that comes up."

"Yeah! Last time we were going to go, Ella had to get sick!" Lucy chimed in angrily. "We were just about to go out the door, and she vomited all over my suitcase!"

"Lucy!" Phoebe reprimanded while Ella's lower lip jiggled. "That's definitely not the way we speak at the table, and we certainly don't make anyone else feel bad for getting sick. You can march right up to your room and forget about dessert!"

Now it was Lucy's turn to hold back her tears as she stomped away from the table.

Matthew, Phoebe's husband, wiped a tear off of Ella's cheek. "Now then, love. Don't get upset over that. These things happen. Nobody's mad at you."

"Lucy is," Ella countered.

"Sisters are usually mad at each other when they're young," Mavis replied, sounding gentler than she normally did. She had a soft spot for her nieces, even if she'd decided to dedicate herself to her career instead of a family or a husband. "They get over all that when they grow up."

"You and Mommy used to fight?" Ella asked.

Phoebe and Mavis looked at each other for a long moment before they fell into a fit of giggles. "Do you remember when you wouldn't let me in your room?" Mavis asked.

"How could I forget? You stole my plastic farm animals and flushed them down the toilet!" Phoebe cackled.

"It got you to come out of your room, didn't it?" Mavis returned. "Yes, Ella, there are lots of times when siblings don't get along. It all works out. Even with mean older brothers like your Uncle Nathan."

"I wasn't mean," Nathan protested. "I just knew what you girls ought to be doing, and you usually weren't doing it at all."

"I guess that means nothing has changed," Phoebe remarked.

Emily sat back, her stomach full and her heart warm as her children reminisced on their younger days. These were the evenings she lived for, when everyone was under one roof. It didn't happen very often, with so many conflicting work schedules or ballet recitals, but she was glad to see that all the hard work she'd put in when they were younger had truly paid off. Now that task was done, she needed to figure out what else she was going to do.

"All right, all right!" Nathan said when Mavis had reminded him of how he'd decided he would teach his younger sisters everything he'd learned in school over the course of a summer. "I just thought you might benefit from it, the same way I think Mom might benefit from a cruise. It'll be relaxing."

"All I've done is relax since I retired," Emily pointed out. "I don't need to go do it somewhere else. I want to actually *do* something, though, so I was thinking–"

"There are lots of places looking for volunteers," Phoebe pointed out as she stepped into the kitchen to grab the pie. "You can make your own hours and volunteer at the humane shelter, or the park, or with some of the local church groups."

Mavis shook her head. "That's a horrible idea. Most of those places are short on volunteers."

Phoebe grabbed a stack of plates from the sideboard. "How is that a bad thing?"

"It means they'll constantly be nagging her and guilting her into putting in more time than she's actually capable of doing," Mavis returned. "I had a friend who did that once. She thought she'd do just a few hours a week with a youth organization, and the next thing she knew she was running the whole thing."

"It doesn't have to be like that." Phoebe, despite being the older sister, had too quiet of a personality to argue with Mavis outright.

Nathan accepted the plate of pie as it was passed around to him. "What she needs is a vacation," he argued. "If she wanted to work, she wouldn't have retired."

Matthew leaned over and cut Ella's share of pie into bites with the side of a fork. "You could always get a part-time job. Some of the shops downtown are looking for clerks, I think."

"And work retail hours?" Nathan exclaimed.

"That is quite enough," Emily began, but she quickly realized that nobody was listening to her. She waited for a lull in the conversation and tried again. "Now, hold on a second…"

but once again they all continued on without her.

"Gran is talking!" Ella screeched, pointing across the table at her grandmother.

Silence descended in the room, followed by laughter.

"Thank you, dear," Emily finally said. "I think I'll have to take some lessons from you. Anyway, what I've been trying to say is that I don't want to take a vacation. I don't want to just sit around knitting, and I think I've been doing nothing but relaxing for months on end. I've still got plenty of years left, and I want to do something meaningful. Volunteering is an interesting idea, and it's one that I'll be keeping in mind. Something I've wanted to do for a long time is to write a book, but I'm a little rusty. I don't even know what I would want it to be about, but I'm not going to just sit around and wait for it to come to me. For now, I think I'd like to start a blog." She smiled as she looked around the table.

The support and encouragement she expected weren't exactly reflected in the faces that looked back at her. They were mostly just stunned, as far as she could tell.

Mavis cleared her throat. "I suppose I could have someone at the office get one started for you."

Emily shook her head. "That won't be necessary."

"But Mom, you don't really know that much about computers," she protested, looking even more flustered. "If you want to have a blog, you have to have a website to host it on. You'd have to build it. There are blogging platforms that streamline that, of course, but you'd still be spending a lot of time on the computer."

Ah, here it was. Her children and many other well-meaning adults in her life had started acting as though she was completely incompetent as soon as she'd retired. While she'd certainly had a hard time when she'd suddenly found herself a widow, that had somehow translated into her being a doddering old fool. "I should remind you that I spent plenty of time on a computer when I was still working at the insurance agency. We might've started out with pencil and paper, but we stayed current with the times."

"It's not the same kind of software," Mavis argued.

"There are videos all over the internet that will show me what I need to do." Emily sat up a little straighter in her chair, glad that she'd taken a moment to do a little research before she'd brought the idea up. There were plenty of people her age who probably didn't bother looking things up for themselves, but she'd found a wealth of information. The truth was that it was probably more information than she could ever sift through, but she was determined to make this happen.

"What's a blog?" Ella asked, a smear of pie on her little cheek.

"Well, dear, it's kind of like a journal. I would write things and put them on the internet where everybody could read them," Emily explained.

Ella's brows scrunched up over her big brown eyes. "I don't know how to read yet."

"That's all right, munchkin. Maybe we can read it to you." Matthew looked to Emily for her approval.

"That sounds like a good plan to me," Emily agreed, pleased to see that at least her son-in-law wasn't staring at her as though she had two heads simply because she wanted to do a little writing.

Nathan cleared his throat. "Mother," he began. He always addressed her more formally when he was about to lecture her. "A blog might sound like just a hobby to you, but these are serious things that people make money doing. You have to have a strategy that would help you gain followers. Quite a few clients have come to me asking for help with just this sort of thing."

Emily leveled her gaze at her son. She loved him, and she was thrilled that he had such a successful career as a marketing consultant, but sometimes she wished he didn't know so much. "I'm not asking for your approval, you know. I'm just telling you that this is something I'm going to be doing."

Genevieve looked at her husband and then at her mother-in-law. "Do you have a focus for your blog, at least? I know a lot of people in the fashion industry who do just that. Why, there's one with a big following that's about nothing but shoes."

That was one thing Emily hadn't really thought about that much. She only knew that she'd wanted to write. Her teachers back in school had always told her she was gifted, and reading had been one of her main hobbies for most of her adult life. But what, exactly, was she going to write about? She'd never be able to convince Nathan or the others that this was just for fun and that it didn't need to be a serious endeavor. Her eyes drifted down to the table, taking in the scraps of food still clinging to the serving dishes, the napkins and silverware, the crumbs that always managed to get everywhere. These were all the signs of a meal well enjoyed. "Food. I'll write about food."

"That sounds like a good idea," Phoebe encouraged. "Everyone loves food."

"I like pie," said a small voice from the kitchen doorway. Lucy stood there, her cheeks stained with tears. "If I apologize to Ella, can I come have some?"

Phoebe smiled at her daughter. "That sounds like a very good solution, my sweet. Come on over."

"There we have it," Emily affirmed. "Food brings everyone together."

CHAPTER TWO

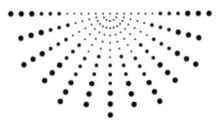

"He would hardly even let me out of the driveway until I promised I'd call him when I needed help getting it monetized." Emily picked up a blue jumper on the clearance rack, considered it for a moment, and then put it back. It didn't look right with her hair color.

"Monetized?" Anita asked, frowning at a scarf with a hem that'd come undone. "What does that mean?"

It was nice to talk to someone else her age. She and Anita had been best friends since high school, and even though they'd had some times where they hadn't always been able to see each other very often, they'd remained close. "I know so little about it that I don't think I even dare explain. Basically, he's insisting that I make money off the thing."

Anita shrugged. "That can't be a bad thing. Neither one of us make very much off our pensions. What do you think of this?" She plucked a purse from a big bin of them.

Emily took in the big gaudy buckles and the heavy zippers. "It's definitely not my style, and it looks like the one you ended up returning last month. You're right, a little extra money is never a bad thing, but this isn't about money. It's about having a purpose in life. I used to feel like I had one, back when I had kids to raise or a job or a husband to take care of." As much fun as Emily always had when she and Anita had a girls' day out, she felt a familiar sadness taking over her. That happened almost every time she thought about her dear Sebastian.

"I know that face." Anita laid a hand on her best friend's arm. "Do you want to go home?"

"Not at all," Emily replied stubbornly, marching with determination over to a display of stockings. She didn't even need any, but she'd look at them to keep herself distracted. "It gets better all the time, but I don't think it'll ever be easy. He was a wonderful man, you know."

"I do." Anita joined her in looking at the stockings, each of them pawing pointlessly through the packages of thin material. "I suppose in that way, I'm pretty lucky."

"How do you mean?" Emily was pretty sure she knew.

"Dan was terrible," Anita said bluntly. "I know you're not supposed to speak ill of the dead and all that, but it's been long enough that I don't think it matters anymore. Besides, I'm only being honest. He was a stubborn old drunk, and his favorite pastime was finding a way to start an argument. Sometimes he'd even argue against something he'd said before, just so he could have an excuse to raise his voice a little. I told him a long time ago he needed to put the bottle down or else he'd end up in an early grave, but he wouldn't listen to me."

Noticing one of the shop girls staring in their direction, she lifted one shoulder slightly in a little shrug. Anita had always been rather loud and rather direct, and there were times when Emily wished she could be the same way. She liked to say she was working on it, but she'd been doing that for decades and she wasn't sure it'd made much difference. "I don't know that I'd call that lucky, dear. I hated to see you go through all that."

They moved on to the rack of new arrivals for spring, bright outfits by current designers that they'd never be able to afford. "So did I, and it was awful in the moment, but you have to admit there's some benefit to it now that he's gone. I can't say that I miss him. The only real adjustment to make was in waking up in the middle of the night and hearing only crickets instead of his snoring. That, or actually being able to talk on the phone without him shouting in the background. Oh, but look at me. I'm not making you feel any better with all this blather."

"It's not that, it's just…" Emily trailed off. Sebastian's death had prompted many thoughts, questions, and feelings. She'd wondered what the rest of their lives might've been like if he hadn't gone on that boating trip, mostly. Emily had reflected many times on how fortunate she'd been to have the time with him that she did, when some people, like Anita, didn't even get that, but that didn't stop the one nagging thought that lingered at the back of her mind. It surfaced every now and then, and she usually just shoved it back down, but it always bobbed right back up.

"What is it?" Anita prompted as she held a skirt up to her waist and checked the length against her legs. She looked up from the swinging floral material and into Emily's eyes, and her face suddenly grew serious. "What's wrong, Em?"

She'd always pictured herself finally saying this, but it was in a lawyer's office or a courtroom, or perhaps even in front of the hearth at home with her children gathered around her. Not in the middle of the store, with a few casual weekday shoppers drifting by and the clerk practically falling asleep at the cash register. This time, though, she couldn't stuff it back down like she normally did. Emily took a deep breath. "I've often wondered if Sebastian's death wasn't an accident."

Anita's shoulders went slack. She put the skirt back on the rack with one hand, but she didn't tear her gaze away from her best friend. "You don't mean that, do you? I mean, you've never said anything about it before."

"Because it's ridiculous, right?" Emily realized just then how much she wanted it to be ridiculous.

"I think you'd better tell me." Anita pulled her purse strap further up on her shoulder and guided Emily by the elbow to the door.

They stepped out into the sunshine, which somehow felt like an even worse backdrop for the things she wanted to say. The cool spring breeze lifted her bright red hair off her neck. Well, it was still mostly red, at least. "It *is* ridiculous, because Sebastian really was a wonderful man. I don't think anyone ever had anything negative to say about him. He was kind and patient. He paid his bills, and he didn't gamble. He always had a steady job, and yet he was a good father. That's not the sort of man that makes enemies."

Anita nodded. "That's true."

"I don't know. I think it's just a feeling more than anything. Besides, Sebastian was an excellent boater. He'd done that sort of thing numerous times. He wasn't like me, no." Emily turned into the next shop simply to get out of that happy sunshine. She did love the outdoors and being in her garden, but right now she found it annoying. She waited a moment, blinking as her vision adjusted to the dark interior of the antique dealer. "I'd slide all over the place, clinging to the rail and waiting for it to be over, no matter how much fun everyone else was having."

Anita slipped her arm through Emily's elbow, holding her up whether she needed or not as they slowly moved past old vases and dusty lamps. "I see. You feel guilty because you decided not to go that day. You think maybe if you'd have been there, things would've been different."

This was exactly why Anita was her best friend. She could be loud and crass, and she often didn't care what anyone else thought, but she always knew exactly what Emily was thinking. Even, as in this case, when Emily hadn't quite realized it herself. "I think you might be right."

Tucking a strand of her pale blonde hair behind her ear, Anita paused next to a display of old records. "Trust me, dear, that's something you'll have to find a way to let go of. I'm not saying it's going to be easy, but Sebastian wouldn't want you to live that way. He'd want to see you happy."

Their attention was distracted by a shout near the front of the store. Both women turned their heads, finding it impossible not to stare as the shop girl behind the counter glared at the young man standing in front of her. "I told you I don't want to talk to you anymore!"

"Come on, Zoe. I said I was sorry." Emily could only see the back of the young man's bald head. He had one earring in, a long one that dangled down. She was fairly certain it was a chain with a skull hanging at the end, a rather distasteful design but the sort of thing young folks liked.

The girl, Zoe, apparently, had thick, dark hair that'd been pulled back into a ponytail that bobbed angrily as she spoke. "Yes, you said you were sorry. You said you were sorry the last time, when you were flirting with Kendra. You said you were sorry lots of times, but it never changes the way you act, does it?"

"Zoe, don't you do this!" He held one long finger out, pointing it right in her face.

Emily tensed. Anita's other arm clamped around her elbow, and the two of them stood locked together as they watched the scene. Emily didn't like seeing how this boy treated her, though she didn't know exactly what she planned to do about it. She had a feeling Anita was reliving her own past with Dan, and she could sense that she wasn't very happy, either.

"Don't do what? Finally break up with you like I should've done ages ago? Why not? Because then I won't have to put up with your awful antics anymore? I've punished myself enough by staying with you, and I'm done! We're over!" She pushed back from the counter, standing as far away from him as she could. It wasn't all that far, considering there were glass display cabinets behind her. Zoe put her chin in the air and folded her arms.

Good for her! Emily thought. She didn't like to see the girl go through this, but she was proud to see her stand up for herself.

Her now-former beau pointed at the front of the building. "If I walk out that door, I'm not coming back. This is it, Zoe. You'll never get another chance. I won't take you back, no matter how much you beg me."

"Trust me, it's not a problem. I look forward to working a shift in peace without you interrupting it." Now she jutted her chin off to the right, pointedly looking away from him.

"Fine!" He stormed out, the bell over the door ringing merrily in contrast to the stormy mood he'd created.

"Well," Anita said, letting out a long breath as she turned into a little aisle crammed with old tea sets. "Things do work out sometimes. I felt like I was watching myself with Dan about forty years ago. I wish I'd have had her bravery. As I was saying, Sebastian would want to see you happy. He'd like the idea of you starting a blog."

Emily nearly forgot what they'd just witnessed at hearing this. A pleasant warmth spread through her. "Do you really think so?"

"Of course, I do! Don't forget that I knew Sebastian just as long as you did." Anita picked up a teacup with little hand-painted scenes on each side and smiled a little as she turned it over in her hand. "He was always encouraging you, and he wasn't the sort to hold you back. I don't think he'd care if it was something in which you made any money, either. He'd just want you to do what you wanted. What's your blog going to be about, anyway?"

"Food," Emily replied, this time feeling much more confidence behind the statement. It didn't hurt that she'd had a day to think about it. "I could go to restaurants and try different foods and write about them. I could even try some recipes and log my experience in that. I could certainly stand a little bit of a change-up from my standard fare. I'm getting bored with making the same things all the time."

Anita set the teacup down with a clack, turning wide eyes to Emily. "You could even try to recreate the dishes you have in the restaurants!"

"I think you have a lot more faith in my cooking skills than I do. Ella said my green beans were yucky."

"That's because your green beans *are* yucky," Anita confirmed with a grin. "Seriously, though! It could be a lot of fun, and everyone loves food. You could do breakfasts, desserts, fast food, fine food, and even an array of dishes all made with the same ingredient. You're not a professional chef, but I think that would just make you more relatable."

Emily shook her finger at her friend. "Now you're starting to sound like Nathan, worried about how I'll engage with my audience."

Anita grabbed her finger and pulled it down playfully. "Only in the interest of you having fun and succeeding at this thing you want to do. Now, let's talk about what you need to get started. Should we head into that little computer shop down the street and get a new laptop for you?"

CHAPTER THREE

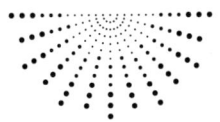

"All right, Rosemary. I've got it all out of the box and plugged in. That wasn't so hard. Let's see what we need to do next." Emily hadn't planned on buying a new computer just for writing. In fact, she figured she'd just used the old, battered desktop in the study, an ancient piece of machinery that would probably work just as well as a boat anchor as a computer. Now that she had the shining new laptop assembled on her dining room table, her stomach swirled with both excitement and nerves.

Rosemary, a fluffy tortoiseshell that Emily had rescued from a shelter a few years ago, sat in the dining chair that Emily had pulled up next to her own. She'd been watching with curiosity as Emily removed the computer and its accessories from the box, and she'd even 'helped' clean up the trash by swiping little bits of plastic and packing foam off the table and onto the floor, taking a placid joy in watching them fall to the rug. Now she turned her big gold eyes to Emily as she talked, but she didn't have any suggestions for how to set things up.

"I just realized something." Emily had started speaking aloud to Rosemary as soon as the cat had come home with her. It just seemed like the right thing to do when the cat would look at her with so much inquiry in her face. The habit had increased once Sebastian was gone and Emily found herself alone in the house. She liked having someone to say good morning and good night to. "I never thought about what kind of software I would need. Can I do this all on the internet? I understand that's how most things are these days. I'm not so far behind the trends that I don't know that, at least."

Rosemary's only response was to carefully groom her whiskers. She licked her front paw and swiped it down the entirety of their length, stretching them until they were straight. When she let go, however, they bounced right back to their wild, every-which-way fashion that they always retained. Emily had found that rather endearing about her. It reminded her of her own wild red hair and how it seemed to have a mind of its own.

"You're right! I just need to turn the thing on and get started. I can watch some of those videos that I found before. That would be the best thing to do. I should probably take some notes, too. I don't fool myself for a moment in thinking I'll actually remember what I'm supposed to do." She found the button that turned the computer on and felt like a success when the screen blinked to life.

As she got up to go find a notepad, her cell phone chirped from her purse. Emily fished it out just in time, answering right before it kicked over to voicemail. "Hello, Phoebe."

"Hi, Mom. How are you?"

Emily frowned as she dug around in the junk drawer for a notepad. "You sound like something's wrong."

"No, nothing's wrong. Lucy, please put your pajamas on. Yes, now. Anyway, nothing's wrong. I just wanted to check in with you and see how you're doing."

"Phoebe, darling. I've known you your entire life, and I can tell when something is wrong. I understand if you don't want to tell me. It might be something that you'd rather keep to yourself. But I do think there's something on your mind."

"Well, yes. There is. I guess I just don't know how I want to say it, because I don't want you to get offended."

Finding the notepad, Emily crossed back over to the dining table and sat down. She stroked her fingers through Rosemary's thick fur. "I've been around a long time, and I try not to get offended by much."

"Well, it's just that I want to offer my help. I could tell you weren't very excited about what Nathan and Mavis had to say about your blog idea. I know how bossy they are, though. Nathan has always acted as though he knows everything, and Mavis does too now that she's been working for that tech firm. In this case they really might know what they're talking about, but I just don't think they always go about it in the right way, and I know I wouldn't want them to give me advice in the same way that they're trying to give it to you, and–"

"You're rambling, sweetheart," Emily said gently. "I'm perfectly aware of what strong personalities they have. Just tell me what you want to tell me, and it'll be perfectly fine."

"All right." Phoebe was silent for a moment. "I might not have the technological or marketing expertise that they do, but I want to offer my help if you need it. I know you don't really like accepting help, and you certainly don't have to, but I'm here if you need me."

Rosemary was purring with delight now. She had one paw resting on Emily's lap, planning to make her way over one foot at a time.

Emily smiled, even though Phoebe wasn't there to see it. Phoebe was the middle child, and she was often a great contrast to her siblings. Emily loved all her children equally but in their own ways. This was exactly what she'd have expected from Phoebe, who always wanted to please. "They both mean well, and you're right. I don't like to accept help from you kids unless I need to move a dresser or something. I admit I very well may need some help, but some of that depends on how this evening goes. Anita and I went down to the computer shop, and I bought a new laptop today."

"You did! How delightful! Good for you!"

Rosemary must've sensed that Phoebe was the one on the line. Now she had two paws in Emily's lap and was trying to rub her cheek against the bottom of the phone.

"I'm excited about it, too. It makes this all feel very official. Anita gave me some great ideas that I can use for the blog when I was discussing it with her, as well. This could really turn into something." Once again she felt that swirl of energy in her stomach, and at the moment it felt much more like excitement than nerves.

"I do hope so. Ella hasn't been able to stop talking about it. I think she feels important because she was there when you brought it up."

Emily leaned down and bumped her nose gently against Rosemary's. "Is that so? I'm so touched!"

"Oh, yes. Now that she knows what it is and that it's all about food, she asks me all the time if you can write about what she's having for breakfast or a snack. She also asked if she could bake cookies with you for your blog."

"My dear heart!" Emily loved her grandchildren more than anything, and it touched her deeply to know they could be so interested in her. "Tell her we will absolutely do that. And, of course, Lucy and I can do something together as well. I wouldn't want her to feel left out."

"I will. Coming, sweetie! Mom, I've got to go. Lucy's ready for bed. But do let me know if there's anything I can do to help you with this. Goodnight."

"Goodnight, dear." Emily hung up, and she felt a warmth in her cheeks. There were some things in her life that weren't perfect. There were days when she missed the regular schedule of having her job at the insurance agency, and of course she missed Sebastian terribly. But she knew without a shadow of doubt that her children loved her. Nathan only gave her his marketing advice because he wanted to see her succeed. Mavis offered to have someone build her website for her because she didn't want her to get frustrated. Phoebe wanted to help in her own way, though she had no idea that the best help she'd given her was motivation. If her granddaughters wanted Emily to do this blog, then by golly, she would!

"All right, Rosemary. We've really got to get started now. Are you comfortable?" The cat was fully in her lap now, positioned so that she faced the computer screen from in between Emily's arms. "I hope you plan to read all the fine print for me."

While Emily had used plenty of computers at work before, they'd always been set up for her. She clicked through various boxes and windows, checked boxes for all sorts of user agreements, and tried to do everything the computer seemed to need. Rosemary was interested in all the clicking and brushed her tickly whiskers against Emily's wrists as she worked.

"I think I'm stuck," Emily finally pronounced. She'd set up the computer, she was fairly sure, although the laptop itself had done most of the work. Now she had to get it hooked up to the internet, and she didn't have a clue as to how to do that. Picking up her phone, she considered giving Phoebe a call. She'd offered, after all, but then Emily noticed how late it'd gotten. "Oh! Rosemary, I think we'd better be getting to bed. The rest will have to wait until the morning."

She scooped up her cat, carrying the fluffball around while she shut off the lights and made sure the door was locked. She passed her knitting basket as she headed toward the stairs. A half-finished scarf stuck out from under the lid. It was a nice way to pass the time, but Emily didn't have any interest in picking it up right now.

"I think I'd much rather be a blogger than a knitter. It sounds more exciting. Don't you think so?"

Rosemary purred happily as they ascended the stairs, and Emily decided to take that as a yes.

As she settled into bed, Emily was content in knowing that she had something to do the next day.

CHAPTER FOUR

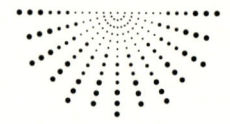

"How many will be dining today?"

Emily beamed at the hostess. She'd put on a new floral dress before heading out to The Silver Swan. It was one of the nicest restaurants in town, and truth be told, it was much nicer than anything she ever would've expected to find in Little Oakley. The village's efforts to spruce itself up and attract tourists and shoppers from other nearby areas had made a difference, though, and The Silver Swan was part of that effort. "Just one, please."

The hostess nodded. "Right this way." She sashayed into the dining area.

Emily paid attention to all of her surroundings. Now that her computer was set up and ready to go, she'd spent some time reading through other blogs that seemed to be similar to the one she wanted to create. One thing she'd noticed was that the writers didn't focus solely on the meal itself when they were eating out. They made notes about the service, the table linens, and the decorations in the restaurant itself. "Atmosphere" was almost always mentioned, and so Emily took note of the big potted palms between the generously sized booths, the decorative silver swans perched on the walls that matched the establishment's name, and even the faint music that was just loud enough to cover the sound of other diner's voices without being too obnoxious.

"Here you are. Your server will be with you in a moment."

Emily sat down, feeling the leather booth squish down comfortably underneath her. She pulled out a pen and a notepad, laying them alongside the napkin and the silverware, prepared to take all her notes down. It would all need to go into the computer later, but she wasn't about to fuss with that when someone might be looking over her shoulder. The only thing she realized she would've liked would be another person to share the meal with so she could discuss the flavors and textures, but she supposed the notepad would simply have to do for now. Maybe that would even be better, so that she could concentrate on her descriptions instead of getting lost in conversation about the weather or family matters. Nearly forgetting she had it, Emily pulled her camera out of her bag and set it alongside the notepad. All the food blogs she'd read included pictures, and she supposed she'd need to do the same. Of course, that would mean learning to take excellent photographs and how to integrate them into each blog post, but that would be a problem for later that night. Or perhaps tomorrow morning.

"My name is Aaron, and I'll be your server this evening." The young man who suddenly stood at the end of the table snapped a pen out from behind his ear and held it above the small pad in his hand. "Shall we start with a drink?"

"Water, please." She didn't want anything to interfere with the flavor profile of her dish. *Flavor profile* was a new phrase to her, but she'd find a way to incorporate it into her writing.

"Very good." Aaron looked slightly cross as he jotted the order down. "And would you like an appetizer to start?"

"No, thank you. I did take a look at your menu online, though, and I'd like to go ahead and order. I'll have the Venetian seafood soup, please." Emily noticed that the young man looked vaguely familiar, but she couldn't quite put her finger on where she'd seen him before.

"A good choice." He noted this and then glanced at the table, taking in the camera and the notepad. "Are you a photographer?"

Emily laughed, feeling a little embarrassed. A part of her wanted the entire world to know exactly what she was doing, and another part of her wanted to keep it a secret until she at least had a nicely polished article ready to go just so she could prove she was capable of doing it. "No, I'm afraid not! This is for my blog, actually. I'll be writing about my meal and your restaurant here."

He stared at her for a long moment. "*You* have a blog?"

She straightened her shoulders and lifted her chin. "I do, actually." It was barely started. She'd entered her email address and chosen a password on a blog platform that a lot of people seemed to be talking about, but she hadn't gotten any further than that. This young man, however, didn't need to know all the details.

The somewhat cranky look returned to his face, and he gestured over his shoulder. "I might have to check with my manager on that. I don't know if they'll allow it."

"Allow it?" Emily was completely taken aback. She'd never given any thought as to whether or not she'd have to ask permission. Besides, who wouldn't want a little bit of free publicity? "I don't see why they wouldn't."

"Fine. Just don't put me in it." He stomped off toward the kitchen.

Aaron's attitude made Emily want to do the exact opposite of what he asked. After all, rude wait staff was certainly part of the experience! She wasn't that sort of person, though. Instead, she glanced around the room. It was dimly lit, part of that atmosphere everyone was always talking about, but it wasn't difficult to spot the head waiter. Most of them were wearing simple, white, button-down shirts, but he wore a dark vest over the top of his. Emily had only to raise a finger and he was at her side in an instant.

"How can I help you, ma'am?"

She spotted his name tag. Calvin was probably in his late twenties. He had dark hair, a very short beard, and kindly eyes. It was obvious right away that he didn't have the same sort of attitude the other young man did. "I just wanted to let you know that your waiter was rather rude to me. I explained to him that I'll be blogging about the meal. I thought it was only fair to let him know, and he seemed upset. Do you have a policy against people reviewing your meals online?"

Calvin's eyes widened a little bit before they narrowed. He glanced toward the kitchen, but there was currently no sign of Aaron. "First of all, we don't have any such policy. We'd be more than happy to hear what you have to say about your experience here. I'm also very sorry to hear that you had a poor experience with your waiter. That's not how we do things at The Silver Swan. I'll speak to him right away."

Emily caught his shirtsleeve just before he turned away. She hadn't received her food yet, and the very man she was complaining about was going to bring it to her. That didn't sound like a very good idea. "No, please don't do that. I just wanted to make sure you were informed."

His dark brows knitted together, but he nodded. "As you wish, ma'am."

With that settled, Emily took some notes while she waited for her food. She picked up her pen and jotted down the quality of the napkin, the cleanliness of the silverware, and even the friendliness of the head waiter. While all of this was fairly new to her, she wanted this first post to be as good as it could possibly be. Maybe she shouldn't have told everyone about her new endeavor. It might've been easier to try her hand at it and see how it went before she made the announcement. When she remembered how excited Ella was, though, she didn't regret a thing.

Emily glanced at her watch. Just how long had it been since she'd ordered? Surely, those folks at the next table had been seated after her. Why were they already eating? It wasn't that Emily didn't understand how things went sometimes in a restaurant. There were some dishes that took longer than others. Things could happen. Maybe her bowl of soup had been spilled, and the waiter had to clean it up. Still, it'd been an awfully long time, and her stomach was starting to rumble. Emily glanced around, but she didn't see any sign of Aaron.

She'd been telling herself she needed to be more assertive, and perhaps now was the time. Emily got up out of her booth, and since there weren't any servers nearby, she walked over to the hostess stand. "I'm so sorry to bother you, but I'm afraid I haven't received my food yet, and I was just wondering–"

"I was just trying to help!"

Emily turned her head toward the kitchen doorway at the back of the restaurant. A large man in a white chef's coat and hat stood just outside it, putting his finger right in Aaron's face. "I didn't ask you to help! That's not your job! It's my job, and you would be smart to remember it."

Aaron's face had gone red, the blush extended to the scalp under his short blonde hair. "Do we really have to do this here?"

The chef was glaring at him, his dark eyes glittering. Clearly, the man didn't care if the entire restaurant witnessed such an argument. "A master does not need a servant to tell him how to prepare an excellent meal. You can stay silent or take your added ingredients to some other kitchen!"

"Oh, my," Emily whispered as she turned back to the hostess.

Calvin showed up just then, looking rather sheepish as he glanced over his shoulder toward the kitchen. He gestured toward Emily's table, gently ushering her back to her seat. "Is there something I can help you with, ma'am?"

"Um…" She'd come in search of her meal, which should've arrived quite some time ago. That would've been a second complaint against the waiter, however, and poor Aaron seemed to be having a bad enough day as it was. "No, that's all right. Thank you."

Calvin moved on and Emily took her seat once again. Her notes were still waiting for her on the table, though they weren't doing her any good without an actual meal to review. She doodled a little in the margins, trying to decide what she should do with herself. Now more than ever she wished she'd brought someone with her so she could at least have a conversation while she waited. Anita, maybe, or Phoebe.

"Here you are." Walking quickly, Aaron dashed up to the edge of her table. He slid a bowl on a plate onto the table in front of her. "Sorry about your wait."

"That's all right, um…" He was turning to leave, but Emily couldn't help but feel sorry for him. She had no idea what might've actually happened in the kitchen, but she couldn't imagine anyone deserved to be reprimanded like that. "Are you all right?"

Aaron's lips were drawn tight into an angry pout, and his shoulders were hunched forward. He glanced toward the kitchen, indicated that he knew exactly what she was talking about. "The chef better watch his back, that's all," he grumbled before he turned and stormed away.

Emily rested her fingers on her collarbone, surprised to hear him speak so bluntly. She followed his back as he retreated toward the service station where the servers prepared drinks and rolled silverware. Calvin approached him, and the two men spoke quietly for a moment. Calvin handed him a dish, and Aaron headed off.

She returned her attention to her meal. A bit of the red broth had been slopped over the side of the bowl. A result, she thought, of Aaron's haste, but not one that she was going to point out to him or even mention in her blog. Instead, Emily wiped it up with the corner of her napkin. Feeling a little self-conscious, she picked up her camera and snapped a few photos. She was no professional photographer, and she'd never done anything more than a few candid family snaps, but the lighting from the window seemed good and the little preview on the back of the camera looked perfectly fine for her purposes. Emily set the camera down and began her meal.

Perhaps it was because she'd waited so long for her food and she was properly hungry. Perhaps it was because she'd been paying so much attention to her surroundings, absorbing every little detail around her. Whatever the reason, the soup was absolutely remarkable! Emily found herself jotting down a note or two after every bite, comparing the seafood soup to both the comforts of home and the joy of an exotic trip. She thought about flavor and texture, and she even paid attention to the fact that the fish had been cut up into perfectly sized pieces that were neither too big nor too small. The tomato-based broth was just salty enough to support the fish without making her reach for her water after every bite. A perfectly crusty piece of buttered bread was served on the plate with the soup, and Emily found it to be an ideal match.

Unfortunately, the bowl of soup was gone before she knew it. Fortunately, the experience had filled up several pages of her notepad. Pleased with the meal and with herself, Emily tucked away her notepad, pen, and camera. There was no sign of Aaron, and so while she waited on him to bring her the check, she got up to find the restroom.

A small sign above a doorway indicated she was heading in the right direction, but Emily found the hallway near the kitchen to be remarkably dark. She fumbled along the wall, searching for the restroom door. If her post was to be about the restaurant itself, then she'd certainly have a lot to say right now. She finally laid her hand on the cold metal of a door latch and pushed.

And found herself standing outside. She'd found the back door to the alley instead of the restroom! Emily was getting irritated now. The experience of her lovely meal was slowly being ruined by everything else going on around her. She was just about to back into the building and shut the door behind her when she realized she wasn't alone.

The waning light of the spring evening was dim back here in the alley, casting everything in a bluish haze. The safety lights overhead had yet to kick on, but there was no mistaking what she saw. Aaron was there, in his black pants and white button-down shirt. He was laying on his side, careless of the dirt or the few bits of trash that hadn't made it into the dumpster. Emily didn't know why, but right away she knew he was dead.

CHAPTER FIVE

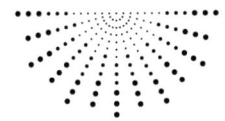

The spinning lights of the emergency vehicles made the exterior of The Silver Swan look like a disco. They'd all arrived very quickly, and she'd be commending them for that if they weren't treating her like she were the victim.

"It's all right, ma'am," Chief Inspector Jack Woods said, speaking to her with far too much patience in his voice. "I'll have someone get you a chair."

"I'm perfectly fine to sit on the curb. Actually, I don't need to sit at all. I'd rather you just listen to me."

He took her by the arm as an ambulance pulled up, bringing her gently toward the back of it. "Don't you worry about anything, ma'am. We'll get it all taken care of. We can always talk later, but right now I think you ought to let these nice people have a look at you. You're a little shaken up."

Yes, she'd certainly been shaken up. It wasn't every day that she found a dead body in an alley, and it was even more disturbing to know she'd seen him alive not long before that. But Calvin had brought her a glass of water, and she'd recovered herself quickly. Now, she was far more concerned with making sure they got her statement, if they wanted it. "They don't need to look me over. I'm fine! The only person they need to be looking at is dead in the alley!"

The paramedics had opened up the back doors of the ambulance, and now the inspector guided her to have a seat inside. He spoke to the one of the EMTs instead of her now. "She was the primary witness, and I think she's a bit rattled. Just make sure she's all right, maybe contact her next of kin to see if they can come pick her up. If not, one of my men will give her a ride home."

"I'm not that frail, and I drove here myself!" she shouted after Woods as he walked away, clearly uninterested in anything she had to say, whether it pertained to his case or not. When it was obvious he wasn't even with earshot anymore, she turned to the paramedic. "Don't you dare call my family! I'm perfectly fine!"

The young man's head bent back at her explosive statement. He nodded and held up a stethoscope. "Could I at least check your vitals, just to keep everyone happy?"

It didn't make her very happy, but Emily couldn't deny that it was a good idea. She let him check her pulse, take her temperature, and then ask her a few questions before he left her to her own devices with a bottle of water.

She sat on the back of the ambulance, perfectly aware that she was pouting like a child and not caring. This had been a horrible start to her food blog! The meal had been excellent, but everything around it had gone completely wrong. There was no telling what her children would think once they got word of this. Nathan would treat her just like Chief Inspector Woods had. He'd probably hire someone to come sit with her during the day, or he'd put her on that blasted cruise ship and insist that she have a good time. Mavis would lecture her about how a blog was too much work. Even Phoebe would have that horribly shocked look on her face, and she'd likely come up with an excuse for Emily to come over and 'watch the children' in the afternoons while she got some things done. So much for doing something with the rest of her life!

"How dare you speak to me like that!" It was the chef again. Now he was standing outside in the parking lot with everyone else, and Chief Inspector Woods was in front of him.

"Sir, it's my job to investigate every potential aspect of this case," Woods replied calmly. "You were this young man's boss, and I understand that you had an argument with him shortly before his death."

Emily felt a grim smile coming over her face. She'd wanted to tell the inspector just that, not because she was convinced the chef had anything to do with Aaron's death but because she knew it was something relevant that should be looked into. She'd watched plenty of murder mystery shows, and she'd even put a few Agatha Christie novels under her belt.

"If you want to talk to anyone, you should be speaking to my silent partner. Marla Burns. That's the one Aaron was always arguing with," the chef insisted.

Woods gestured for one of the other officers to contact her before he turned back to the chef. "We'll do that, but I'd still like to hear what happened between yourself and this young man. Could you tell me more about the argument, please?"

"Yes!" the chef bellowed, flinging his hands in the air. "You could say it was an argument, but I was really just reprimanding him! He had no idea of his proper place in a kitchen! It was his job to take the orders and serve the food. He had only to pick up the dishes and take them to the customers! That was it! Could he stick to that? No!"

Woods took a step back to avoid the man's angry gestures, but he wasn't done with the chef yet. "Would you mind explaining to me exactly what the problem was?"

The chef snatched his hat off with one hand and ran the other through his sweaty hair. "That insolent boy was constantly trying to offer improvement to some of the best dishes in the house! Dishes that I created myself, ones that our customers loved and always raved about! He had no business sticking his nose into any of the food, other than to bring it to the diners!"

"I see." Woods was making notes. "And that made you angry?"

The chef's face was the color of a beet now. "He had some audacity to question my menu! Of course, it made me angry! But angry enough to fire him, not to kill him! There would never even be a chance for me to do such a thing! You can ask the other cooks!"

Woods gave him a serious look, suggesting he'd be doing just that.

A sedan screeched into the parking lot. A woman about ten years younger than Emily leaped out of the driver's seat, smoothing the wrinkles out of her pale pink skirt suit. "I'm Marla Burns. I'm the owner. What's happening here?"

"Half-owner," the chef corrected.

Emily guessed that someone else must've already called Ms. Burns, or else she wouldn't have gotten here so quickly. Chief Inspector Woods dismissed the chef and brought Marla around the side of the building, further from the alley. That meant they were also closer to the ambulance, and Emily had no problem hearing the entire conversation. She sipped her water as she listened to the inspector explain what'd happened.

"That's my son!" Marla screeched, putting her head in her hands. "Oh, not Aaron! I bet it was that awful Chef Jaubert!"

Emily's heart broke for her, and she nearly got up and left. She didn't want to be a witness to such grief. Her curiosity took over, though, as the inspector began asking questions.

"I'm so very sorry. I know this is a difficult thing for you, but I do need to ask you a few things. Why do you think Chef Jaubert would want to harm your son?" Woods was speaking with a calm patience, as befit the situation, but

Emily noted that he wasn't condescending to Marla as he'd been to her.

Marla sniffled and tried to tell her story. "This business belonged to my husband and me, you see. It was a family restaurant, and we had great aspirations for it. Aaron always had dreams of taking it over one day. That changed when my husband passed away." Marla paused as she sniffled some more. "He was sampling a dish. He was an excellent chef, and he always made sure that his creations were as perfect and tasty as possible. He didn't realize he was allergic to some of the nuts in the dish, however. I hired Chef Jaubert to replace him. He was very well known for his work at The Sapphire Hummingbird, and I just wanted to keep the restaurant open in my husband's memory."

"Mm hmm." Woods was writing quickly as he listened.

"We fell on hard times," Marla continued. "It's not easy to keep a restaurant going, you see. I wound up selling half of the business to

Jaubert, because I had no choice. I couldn't even afford to pay him otherwise. Aaron had been angry with me ever since, because he knew it meant he'd never get to take over the way he wanted to. There was much here at The Silver Swan that I didn't have any control over."

"I see. And so that would explain why Aaron was trying to tell Jaubert how to do his job?" the inspector asked.

"Quite likely," Marla admitted quietly.

Emily took another sip of her water and looked away when she saw Woods turn his gaze toward her. The story was an interesting one, and she found herself wanting to know more about it. Why would a chef buy out half of a restaurant that was struggling to pay its bills? And why would Aaron have been a server instead of the head waiter or a cook if his own mother owned half of the place? If it was because of his dour attitude, then she certainly understood. Or perhaps that was one of the things about The Silver Swan that she hadn't been able to control.

Aaron himself seemed rather out of control. It sounded as though he and Jaubert had argued other times before. Perhaps his personality kept him from climbing higher within the business more than anything. Even so, would Jaubert go to such lengths to get rid of him? It wasn't good for business to have a dead body in the alley, no matter what the cause.

"Ma'am?"

Emily found a young woman looking at her expectantly. She hadn't seen her yet, but given her uniform she was obviously with the police. "I suppose you're here to tell me I need to lie down? Or that you think I might be having a heart attack because of what I saw?" she asked sassily. "Perhaps you've come to check me into a nursing home?"

The young woman blinked in surprise. "No, actually. I was just seeing if there was anything you needed. I'm DC Bradley. You can call me Alyssa, if you'd like."

She might've been a little hasty in the way she'd addressed this young woman, but given how everyone else here had been treating her, Emily wouldn't have been surprised if DC Bradley had been sent over here to drive her home and tuck her into bed. "That's very kind of you. I'm afraid there's not much you can do for me. I'm just an old woman."

"But I understand you were the one who found the victim," Alyssa insisted as she sat down on the back of the ambulance next to her. "Did you get a chance to give your statement?"

Emily took in the young woman's dark hair, pulled back tightly under her bowler, and her bright eyes. She looked genuinely interested in anything Emily might have to say. Of course, now that most of it had come out already, she didn't feel that her statement was all that important. "I'm afraid I don't have anything new for you, dear. I only know that the young man argued with the chef, and I think all of Little Oakley knows about that after his rather loud interview."

DC Bradley put a hand over her mouth to suppress a giggle. "You might be right about that."

There was something about her that Emily immediately liked, and she patted Alyssa's knee. "Then I think you already know everything I do. I came here on a misguided idea to start a food blog. I just wanted to have a nice bowl of the seafood soup, which was excellent, by the way, and I wound up finding much more than I bargained for."

"You're starting a blog?" Alyssa's eyes went wide.

Oh, here it went again. Another young person who was about to tell her she wasn't capable of such forward-thinking, technological things. "That's what I'm trying to do, yes."

"That's wonderful!" DC Bradley enthused. "A friend of mine does that. She writes book reviews, mostly. She wants to be a published author, someday, so that's where she's starting for now. I don't think I have the patience for it, myself, but I do enjoy reading what she writes. I guess your blog is about food?"

Emily smiled, feeling a spark of pride. "That's the plan. I don't officially have it started, yet. This was supposed to be my first post. I've got all sorts of notes, too." She pulled the notebook out of her bag and looked at it glumly. "It might all be a waste, now. I'm not sure I can write about any of it."

"Your handwriting is beautiful."

This young lady was just full of compliments and zest, something Emily hadn't expected but was pleasantly surprised to find. "Why, thank you."

"I'm sure your blog is going to be wonderful, even if things went disastrously here today. Well, disastrous for everyone else but people in my line of work. If nothing ever happened, I wouldn't have much to do. I'd like to be the chief inspector one day." Alyssa looked over at Woods, who was pointing his finger and ordering other officers around.

"That's quite the goal, and you're well on your way, if you ask me," Emily said with a smile. "You're already much better at talking to people than he is. You'd have thought I was an escapee from a nursing home, the way he treated me." She felt herself get a bit bitter all over again.

Alyssa shook her head. "He's like that, sometimes. His mother is older and rather frail, and I think he sees other people in that light, too."

"Well, I suppose I can forgive him for that. Mostly." She was still miffed by the fact that he'd refused to listen to her. What if his poor mother had something to say? Would he have just shuffled her off on a medic?

"I think things are just about wrapped up here for now, so you should be fine to go home," Alyssa said, looking around.

Emily noted that she didn't ask her if she needed someone to call her children to come and collect her, and she appreciated it. In fact, she was pretty certain she wasn't even going to tell her children, just so they wouldn't' have any more cause for concern than they already thought they did. "Thank you. I think I'll do that. I'll have to run in and pay for my meal, though. I'm afraid I never did get the check in all that confusion."

"If you think of anything pertinent to the case, or even if you just want to tell me more about your blog, here's my number." Alyssa produced a card from the pocket of her vest and handed it over.

Emily accepted the card and tucked it into her bag. There was just something about this girl that she liked. "Thank you very much, dear. I appreciate that."

CHAPTER SIX

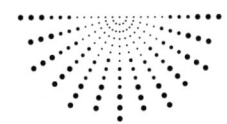

"I know, darling. I'd planned a nice long day at home in front of the computer. You would've liked that, and I'm sure you would've been a great help." Emily stood near the front door, buttoning up her raincoat and making sure she had an umbrella with her. It turned out that the disaster at The Silver Swan had messed with not only her dinner plans but her entire schedule for the next day. She'd intended to take all her notes and turn them into her first official post while everything was still fresh. In light of the fact that someone had died, she wasn't sure she felt all right about actually using the material.

Rosemary sat at the edge of the rug, letting out a small meow as she watched her owner get ready to head out.

"You know, you might actually be rather happy by the time I get back," Emily replied. "I thought it might make an even more interesting article if I tried to reproduce the soup from the restaurant. Anita said that whole thing about how cooking myself without being a professional would make people relate to my writing, or something like that. Besides, there are already tons of other bloggers who are simply reviewing restaurant food, so it might be more fun to do it this way."

The cat picked up one paw, holding it in the air in front of her. That was a habit of hers that Emily had noticed shortly after she'd adopted her. At first, Emily had worried there was something wrong with her paw. She'd even taken her to the vet for it, concerned there was a thorn buried between the cat's paw pads that Emily hadn't been able to locate. The vet hadn't found anything, either. It was only after she paid for that unnecessary visit that Emily noticed Rosemary switched off which paw she held up. It was just an affectation Rosemary had, and a rather cute one as far as Emily was concerned.

"Anyway, it was a seafood soup. You'll be around to help clean up the leftovers."

Rosemary let out another meow, her big gold eyes curious.

"That's my girl. You watch the house for me, and I'll be back as soon as I can." She stepped out the front door and pulled up her hood as she headed down the walkway to her car. "Of course I had to pick the rainiest day this week to go out!"

It turned out she wasn't the only one who'd decided to get her shopping done. Quite a few other customers were heading into the supermarket, grabbing carts, and diving into the aisles for the best deals that they could find. Living alone meant that Emily was never too concerned about her grocery budget, even if she was living on a fixed income. Young families had to spend a rather large portion of their paychecks at the grocery store, but she could usually get away with fairly little. As far as she was concerned, that meant she was perfectly justified in buying a few special ingredients for this recipe.

If only she could find them. Carrots and celery were easy enough, and they were on her list regardless. But Emily found herself standing in front of a large walls of greens, feeling more overwhelmed than the very first time her mother had sent her out for groceries alone. There were some ingredients that she was just so used to picking up, and others that she'd apparently never paid attention to.

"Can I help you find something?" A young man in a blue apron approached her from over near the potatoes. He had tattoos up both arms and bright green hair that certainly wasn't natural.

Emily shook her head. She'd been shopping here for years, and she really shouldn't need any help with this. All she had to do was look harder. She didn't want to accept help from anyone unless she truly needed it, or else everyone she met out in public was going to start treating her the way Chief Inspector Woods had. Some young man like him, with all his wild fashion trends, probably didn't want to help an old lady anyway. The thing was, she'd already been standing in the produce section for five minutes, and she hadn't yet found what she needed. "I suppose so. Do you know if you have fennel bulbs? I do sometimes buy fennel seeds over by the dry spices, but I don't see the bulbs." She didn't even know what they looked like.

His mouth split in a friendly grin. "Fortunately, I usually stock this section. Otherwise, I don't think I'd have a clue what you're talking about," he said with a laugh. He reached up toward the top of the shelves and lifted down a fat, pale bulb topped with greens. "This looks like a good one. Can I put it in a bag for you?"

"That would be wonderful, thank you." Emily felt ashamed of herself for assuming that he wouldn't be helpful simply because he looked like the sort who would be smoking out back instead of doing his job.

"Can I ask what you're making with it?" he said as he expertly popped it into a bag, twisted the top into a little knot, and put it on the scale. "I'm not much of a cook, and when I see people using things I don't know anything about, I like to ask them."

She squinted to see the tag on his apron, which told her his name was Toby. Emily couldn't be sure that Toby wouldn't deride her for wanting to write a food blog, just as Aaron had, but he'd already shown that he could be kind. He'd also told her a little bit about himself by admitting he didn't cook much, and so it only felt right to tell him. "I'm making a Venetian seafood soup. It's for the food blog I'm starting."

"Really?" He bobbed his head eagerly. "That's so cool! I'd love to do something like that, but I don't think I have anything worth writing about. What I'd really like to do is get my music out there. My buddies and I have a band, and we're pretty good, but we've got to get some good recording equipment first. Anyway, is there anything else you need for your recipe?"

Emily looked over her list for anything else that she wouldn't normally buy. "Here's one that I can promise I've never had to find before: bottled clam juice."

"Ew!" Toby laughed. "I guess that makes sense in a seafood soup, though. I think that's right over here."

"Tell me a little more about your band," Emily said as they headed down the aisle.

Toby flapped his hand in the air dismissively. "I don't think it's the sort of thing you'd like."

"You listened to me about my blog," she pointed out.

"All right. We're a typical rock band, but we like to incorporate some classical instruments into our music, too. I've got a friend who plays the French horn, and then another one who plays the violin. I know some bands already do that, but we just want to find ways to blend different kinds of music together," Toby explained.

Emily didn't really know a thing about music, but she felt good in showing Toby that she cared. That was all anyone in the world really needed sometimes. "That sounds very interesting."

"We think so," Toby agreed. "Hopefully we'll be getting some gigs soon. Here. I think this is what you're looking for. There are a few different kinds."

She plucked a bottle from the shelf that she thought looked big enough and then checked her list again. "I think I'm down to just the seafood itself. Do you know if you have a good selection of fresh fish?"

Toby shrugged. "I don't know, exactly, but I can show you what another customer taught me a while back." He guided her over to the frozen section. "Like I said, I don't cook a lot. But people come in and they talk about what they're making, and I really try to listen. This one lady was making seafood linguine for a big dinner party, and she said it was a lot easier to buy this frozen mix."

"I never thought about that. Most of the fish I've prepared were ones my husband caught while on a trip." She'd been so used to fresh fish, at one point both she and Sebastian had both gotten sick of eating it.

He opened one of the freezer doors. "It's in the bag right there. I'd grab it for you, but I'm allergic to shellfish. I have to be kind of careful."

"Oh, my!" Emily wouldn't want her little hobby to interfere with this nice young man's life, and so she quickly reached for the bag herself. A lightbulb went off in her mind as she thought about food allergies, and she stored it away as something to possibly talk to Anita about when she got home. "Are you allergic to anything else?"

"Not that I know of," Toby replied with a shrug as he shut the freezer. "I was worried I wouldn't be able to work here because of it, but they said they'd accommodate me. I wear gloves when they put me on the cash register just to be safe. Is there anything else on your list?"

"I think I'm all good. Thank you so much for all your help. And good luck with your band!"

"Good luck with your blog, too!" he returned. "I hope I get to read it someday."

Smiling, Emily headed toward the checkout. She paused on the way for a few treats for Rosemary so she wouldn't feel left out.

However, by the time she got home and started her cooking, the cat wasn't interested at all in any prepackaged treats from the supermarket. She knew that her owner had something far more interesting up on the counter, and she flicked her fluffy tail against Emily's ankle.

"I know," Emily replied as she got out her favorite pots and pans and laid out the recipe on the counter. She'd printed it off the internet from her new laptop, since her own cookbooks didn't have anything quite that exciting in their pages, and now she could only hope that it was a good one.

Rosemary was even more insistent as Emily unpacked her grocery bags. There were a few items that needed to go into the refrigerator or the cabinets, but most of what she'd purchased was for this recipe and so went on the counter. Rosemary stood up on her hind legs and stretched her front paws as far up as she could, nearly reaching Emily's hip.

"You silly girl!" Emily cooed, gently prying Rosemary off of her. "I'll give you a bite later. I haven't even opened the package yet, and already you can smell it. No wonder Toby was hesitant to pick it up."

She continued to think about the young man as the grocery store as she filled a pot of water to boil the shrimp in. It had to be very difficult for him to keep his job there if he had a severe allergy like that. He'd have to be vigilant all the time, ensuring that he didn't even accidentally pick up a bag of seafood. It would probably be much easier for him to just get a job somewhere else, but instead he'd chosen to work there.

She put a lid on the pot of water and turned up the heat. Anybody who worked around food would have to be extremely aware of food allergies, and that would be even more difficult in a restaurant where things weren't prepackaged and labeled. Aaron's father had died of an allergic reaction. What about Aaron? Could he have the same nut allergy? And if he did, then why wouldn't he have been more careful? It seemed she had far more questions than answers when it came to this, and it was difficult to think about. Emily felt bad for everyone involved, and yet she had to wonder if it was truly an accident.

As she chopped the carrots, celery, onions, and even the fennel bulb, Emily realized how simple it would be to slip something into a meal if she were the chef and she wanted to poison someone. Depending on how sensitive the allergy was, only a small bit of nuts or oil or whatever the offending food could be easily disguised. Even the dish she was making right now, with its tomato-based broth, could suddenly end someone's life if they didn't know what was in it.

"Meow?" Rosemary asked, watching carefully as Emily put all the chopped vegetables in a skillet with a tiny bit of oil. She excitedly dove after a tiny bit of onion that slipped off the cutting board and bounced onto the floor, and she was rather disappointed when she discovered it wasn't a bite of fish.

"I know. I was thinking that, too," Emily admitted. "Aaron caused trouble at The Silver

Swan for Chef Jaubert. He couldn't fire him, because that would probably be the one thing his silent partner would be willing to argue with him about. But kill him? That might actually be easier. As soon as I get this simmering, I'll have to give that Alyssa girl a call."

CHAPTER SEVEN

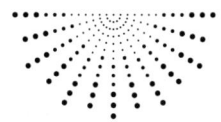

"Thanks for coming with me." Emily turned off the engine and checked her hair in the rearview mirror. She'd carefully styled it, but her wild curls didn't much care. They were already working loose from her updo, and by the time the event was over, she'd look like she'd been out for a stroll on a windy day instead of at a much more formal event.

"Oh, sure." Anita patted her short blonde hair into place, although it was never really out of place to begin with. It seemed to just go right where she wanted it as soon as she got out of bed in the morning, at least to Emily. "I can never resist a good funeral."

Giving up on her hair, Emily opened her door and climbed out. She ignored Anita's joke for the moment. "I just felt as though I had to come. I didn't know him at all, but given that I was the one who found him in the alley, it just seemed..."

"Appropriate?" Anita filled in, her heels clacking on the pavement. "I can certainly understand, and that's exactly why I'm here. I didn't know him, either, and I'm sure I could find much more exciting things to do today. But it only seems appropriate to accompany my best friend to such an awkward event, and therefore I'm happy to do so."

The breeze flipped a stray strand of hair into Emily's face, and she forcefully tucked it behind her ear as they approached the funeral parlor. "It could end up being more interesting than you think."

"How's that?" Anita flicked an invisible speck of lint off her dress.

"I was thinking about everything I overheard while people were being interviewed. It turns out that Aaron's father died due to a nut allergy he didn't know about. I have to wonder if something similar happened to him."

Anita pursed her lips. "It seems a little unlikely that father and son would die of the exact same thing."

"Yes," Emily agreed. "But I'm saying it could be the same thing in different circumstances. His father's death was an accident, but what if Aaron's wasn't? The chef he worked for wasn't very pleased with him, and he even told Chief Inspector Woods that he'd thought about firing Aaron. I saw the two of them fighting, and it sounded as though it was the sort of thing that happened all the time." She hadn't been able to stop thinking about her theory, and she'd even managed to spend a few minutes on the phone with Alyssa to go over it. DC Bradley didn't seem quite as convinced, but she did say she'd take notes and look into it.

"I thought you were supposed to be blogging about food, not murder mysteries," Anita said with a smile.

"Perhaps I'll have to start a second one," Emily replied indignantly. They entered the front door of the funeral parlor and joined the queue. "I have a few other ideas, too."

"Oh?" Anita raised an eyebrow.

Emily glanced around. This certainly wasn't the right time to be discussing it, not when the deceased was in the next room and all these folks had come to mourn him. But she had to tell someone! "His mother didn't sound very pleased with him, either."

Anita's brow crinkled. "Surely his own mother wouldn't kill him!"

"I hope not," Emily quickly agreed. "I just know that he was angry with her for selling half of the restaurant to Chef Jaubert."

"Then why didn't Aaron kill her?" Anita challenged as she paused to sign the guest book. "Or for that matter, why didn't he kill the chef and get that half of the restaurant back? Oh, I don't even know why I'm signing this. Nobody will know who I am! Here." She thrust the pen into Emily's grasp.

Emily knew that her name had some possibility of being recognized by the deceased's family, but it didn't bother her. "I don't have any of the answers, but I'm finding myself speculating about them. I guess finding a dead body will make you want to know a little more than you do. I don't advise it, though."

"How did your kids handle it when you told them?"

Setting down the pen for the next person, Emily frowned. "I didn't, actually. I decided it was easier not to have to worry about their reactions. I saw the way the chief inspector looked at me, like I was some delicate flower that was going to fall apart if it was so much as looked at the wrong way. I didn't need to get that all over again."

Anita stood sideways in the line so she could still look at her friend, and now she gave her a wry smile. "So instead of telling them just a little bit, you're going to wait until you have a whole story?"

"I suppose so," Emily agreed, smiling herself. "They won't have a chance to worry about me once they realize I've got the whole thing handled."

"Brave of you."

"Or I'm just avoiding the inevitable. It works for me either way, for the moment." Emily noticed they were getting closer to the casket. No matter how many funerals she'd been to over the years, this part never got any easier. It was always a little disturbing, but she tried her best to brace herself. The very last thing she needed was to faint or have any other response that would give anyone cause for concern. Fortunately, Aaron's immediate family seemed busy enough accepting condolences from other people they knew, so she didn't have to worry about explaining herself. She took a deep breath, straightened her shoulders, and stepped up to the casket behind Anita.

Emily blinked. She looked up at the wall and then back down, trying to make sure she saw what she thought she saw. Nothing had changed, and she hadn't imagined it. "Do you see that earring?"

"What about it?"

The other visitors were coming up behind them now, and so they turned down the far aisle of the room. "He wasn't wearing it when he was working at The Silver Swan?"

Anita shook her head, not understanding. "So? At an upscale place like that, I wouldn't be surprised if they made him take it out."

That was all very reasonable, but it wasn't the point. "I didn't recognize him until I saw him wearing the earring."

"Oh, honey." Anita took her by the shoulders and steered her toward a chair. "Let's find you a place to sit down. I think maybe this is harder on you than you thought."

"No, you don't understand!" Emily dug in her heels, turned around, and pulled Anita with her toward the back of the room. "I've seen him before, even before I saw him at The Silver Swan. And so have you! I just didn't realize it until now. I think he's the same young man who was arguing with the girl behind the counter at the antique shop." Her body was shaking, but it was due to the jolt of adrenaline that'd just shot through her.

"We only saw the back of his head," Anita argued, but she looked toward the front of the room uncertainly. "Are you sure?"

Spotting the latest arrival to the funeral, Emily knew for certain. "I am now. Look. There's the shop girl herself!"

They both watched as the girl from the antique store stepped into the room. She looked appropriately sad. Or perhaps, Emily thought, she just looked grim. Her mouth was a hard line that turned down a bit at the ends. She didn't even glance in the casket or stop to speak to Aaron's mother. Instead she waved to someone who was already seated. Emily's eyes quickly darted to the left to see who, and her mouth fell open when she saw it was Calvin.

"Do you see him? The one she's sitting with?" Emily asked, barely restraining herself from pointing. "He's the head waiter at The Silver Swan! What if she killed Aaron so she could date Calvin instead?"

"With the way he was treating her at her place of work, it seems to me she had reason to kill him anyway," Anita noted. "I was a little concerned for her since he was being so aggressive."

Emily moved across the back of the room and started up the center aisle, dragging Anita along with her.

"What are we doing?" her friend asked quietly, trying not to get the attention of the other mourners.

"Getting more information," Emily replied simply. She had just as much right to be here as anyone else, and other than the first couple rows of seating that were reserved for immediate family, it didn't matter where they sat.

Making their way around a few other people, Emily managed to get two seats right behind the shop girl and Calvin. She waggled her eyebrows at Anita, feeling successful, but Anita looked like she was going to be sick. Emily sat anyway.

The two young people in front of them paid no attention to who was sitting behind them. Emily felt a moment of triumph when she saw

Calvin reach over and take the girl's hand. "Are you holding up all right?"

"Well enough," she replied, bitterness evident in her voice. "It's kind of unreal."

Calvin looked up toward the casket and nodded his head. "I know. I'm sorry you're having to go through all this. It can't be easy for you."

She let out a long, shuddering sigh. "I thought it would be harder, actually."

Emily nudged Anita and wiggled her eyebrows once again, getting excited. The two of them were obviously in cahoots over Aaron's death. They wanted him out of the picture, perhaps so they could date and also perhaps because he hadn't been a very good boyfriend. This was all the evidence Emily needed, and she'd be calling Alyssa as soon as she had the chance.

"Did you talk to Mom?"

Emily blinked and her shoulders sagged when she heard Calvin ask this question.

"For a little bit," the girl replied with a nod. "She said she'll be coming back from her business trip in a few days, and she felt bad that I was still taking care of Ralph even with all this going on. I told her I didn't mind, and that it was actually kind of nice to be able to spend a little more time at home right now."

"Brother and sister," Emily mouthed, and Anita nodded.

She sat listening to them for several more minutes, hearing talk of grocery shopping, running errands, and making sure their mother's mail was picked up. None of it was very consequential, and it didn't prove anything as far as what had actually happened to Aaron. Their relationship wasn't what she'd expected, but it still thickened the plot as far as Emily was concerned. She wished she had her notepad with her so she could write it all down, but for now she'd just have to memorize as much of it as possible before she chatted with her new friend on the police department.

CHAPTER EIGHT

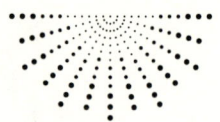

"All right. How long am I supposed to leave this in the oven?" Emily squinted at her latest recipe. It was another one she'd found online for seafood casserole, and it sounded like a good idea since it would allow her to use up some of the seafood that hadn't been used in the soup. She was never one to waste if she could help it, and this would give her another thing to write about for her blog. Unfortunately, the print had come out extremely small this time, and she had to tilt her head back and squint just to read it. She had a feeling she'd either missed an ingredient or done something wrong, but she couldn't be sure just what.

Rosemary sat in a kitchen chair nearby. It'd been a compromise the two of them had reached earlier. The cat had been absolutely fascinated by the smell of her cooking. It was adorable, but it'd become a problem as she kept standing up on her hind legs and trying to reach Emily's hands or what was on the counter. Emily thought she'd managed this problem by gently prying her off and shooing her away, but Rosemary had been insistent. If she couldn't reach for the yummy smelling things, then she would just jump right up on the counter and take them for herself! After she'd run off with a whole shrimp, Emily had brought in the kitchen chair and made a spot for the cat there, where she could occasionally give her a tidbit of food. Maybe it wasn't really a compromise as much as it was a war treaty, but Emily did like having someone to talk to.

"It doesn't smell very good, does it?" she asked as she peeked into the oven. "Never mind. I'm not sure why I asked you that. You'd eat it regardless, wouldn't you?"

Rosemary jumped down to have a sniff at the open oven door, but Emily gently pushed her away with her foot before she had the chance to burn her crazy little whiskers.

A knock at the door made Emily jump. She slammed the oven door. "Are you coming with me to see who it is, or are you going to stick around here until my back is turned?"

The cat gave one last glance at the oven before she was at Emily's heels.

"Good. That works for me." Emily went to the door, expecting it to be someone selling things or perhaps one of her children. Instead, she found DC Alyssa Bradley standing on the stoop. Her heart gave a little jump. "Alyssa! What a surprise!"

"I'm sorry for the intrusion," the young woman began. She knitted her fingers together in front of her, seemed to understand how it looked, and then forced her hands to her sides. "I can come back another time if you'd like, but I had a few things I wanted to discuss with you. Things I'd rather not discuss over the phone."

Emily caught her meaning immediately. She held the door open wide and waved her inside. As she did so, she realized just how her house looked. Emily's current interest in her food blog meant that she'd neglected the rest of her house. The rugs hadn't been vacuumed, and a basket of towels sat next to the sofa waiting to be folded. A fine layer of dust had settled over the television. "Come in. I'm sorry about the mess."

"Oh, there's nothing to worry about." Alyssa stepped inside and immediately bent down to hold her hand out. "Who's this pretty little girl?"

Rosemary must've understood what she said, because she immediately rubbed the side of her face on Alyssa's fingers.

"This spoiled little princess is Rosemary." Emily always enjoyed introducing her cat to new people. She thought the cats' reaction said a lot about the person, and it was clear that Rosemary approved of Alyssa. "I pay the mortgage, but she's the one who actually rules the place."

"I don't doubt that for a second," Alyssa laughed as Rosemary bumped her head up against her palm. Regretfully, she stood up and left the cat to her own devices. "I appreciate your time today, Mrs. Cherry. I need to talk to you about Aaron Burns' death.

Emily's heart did another little jump, even though she'd had a good idea that was exactly what Alyssa would want to talk about. Unfortunately, she already had a lot on her mind considering the concoction she currently had in the oven. To top things off, it smelled like it was burning. "Would you mind stepping into the kitchen with me? I've got to check on the casserole, although I'm afraid of what I'm going to find."

"Of course. Anything you need."

The kitchen was even more of a mess than the living room, a fact that Emily hadn't quite realized until she came in through the doorway and could take it all in at once. She'd been concentrating so much on getting the dish put together that she hadn't bothered to put her ingredients away as she went. The container of cream, the bag from the seafood, and the remaining block of cheese were all still sitting out on the counter alongside the castoffs from the celery and onion. She'd spilled a bit of flour and salt, and just about every dish in the house seemed to be piled in the sink. "I'm so sorry for this mess. Here. You can have a seat right here while I get working on things." Emily swiped a few things away from the breakfast bar.

"Thank you." Alyssa sat on the offered stool, and Rosemary jumped up onto the one next to her.

"You mind your manners, young lady," Emily said to the cat. "Now then, I'm dying to hear what you have to say. Oh, no. I suppose that's not the right way to phrase that."

Alyssa laughed. "It's perfectly fine. We get jokes like that all the time, and sometimes we even make them ourselves. There was a break in the case, though, and I wanted to make sure you were one of the first to know before it went out to the media."

Emily grabbed a potholder and looked in the oven, but her mind was hardly on the dish at all. She noticed that the grated parmesan cheese on top was a bit burned, but she didn't care very much as she pulled it out and set it on a cooling rack. "I don't know if I want you to tell me I was right or if I'd rather hear that I was wrong," she admitted, frowning down at the casserole.

"It was a little bit of both," Alyssa admitted. "Would you rather sit down to talk about it?"

"No, no." If anyone else had asked her that, Emily might take offense. She'd had far too many people worrying about her state over the past week or so, fussing over whether she was doing too much or if she could handle whatever it was that she wanted to do. There was something different about Alyssa, though, much more respectful and understanding. "I think I'd rather clean up so that at least I have something to do with my hands. It isn't as though sitting down and staring at you is going to change the news, is it?"

"I'm afraid not," Alyssa acknowledged. "I suppose I should start with Aaron's mother. After my discussion with you, I was able to arrange a rather lengthy interview with her. She presents herself as being rather wealthy and high-class, but she's actually kind of a mess. She's had a very difficult time ever since her husband died, and our financial investigation shows that she really has had a hard time keeping The Silver Swan open. It didn't even improve all that much once she sold half of the place to Chef Jaubert. It saved her from having to pay his rather lavish salary, but it looks like there's quite a bit that goes into running a place like that."

Emily nodded as she put the cream and cheese back in the fridge, thinking of just how much she'd spent at the grocery store on the ingredients for just a couple of meals. "I'm sure that's true."

"As for Aaron," Alyssa continued, "he found out he had a peanut allergy after his father's death. Our medical examiner explained to me that these types of allergies can come on in adulthood, so even if you grew up eating peanut butter your entire life you could still turn around one day in your twenties and suddenly be allergic. It sounds like Aaron's father had an incident like that, and so he got himself tested. Once he knew, he was very careful to stay away from them. There were a few dishes served at the restaurant that were made with them, though."

Grabbing a rag, Emily started wiping down the counters. Her feelings were mixed. She didn't want anyone to have been murdered.

The idea was horrible, of course. At the same time, she'd feel very silly if she'd made such a fuss over what turned out to be an accidental ingestion of peanuts. Aaron had been angry that day, and maybe he wasn't as careful as he should've been.

Alyssa was absently petting Rosemary now, who was encouraging her with tiny meows. "It might've been written off as a simple accident, if it weren't for the fact that you'd witnessed Aaron fighting with his girlfriend. Her name is Zoe Poole."

"The one who works at the antique shop, right?" Emily realized she'd wiped the same spot on the counter about twenty times now and forced herself to move on.

"That's the one," Alyssa said with a nod. "The two of them had broken up right before Aaron's death. That did make her a suspect, but she was at work the day he died. She was clocked in and on camera, so there's really nothing she could've done."

"I see." Emily reached the end of the counter. She still had to clean up all the dishes, but those could wait. It would be rude to do that much washing up while she had company, right?

"However, it was easy to confirm your suspicion that Zoe and Calvin were brother and sister. I was able to find that out with a very simple search of public records, and I went to talk to him. He was actually how Zoe and Aaron had met in the first place. Zoe had come into The Silver Swan at one point to drop something off to her brother, Aaron was there, and the two of them began dating. Calvin knew how poorly Aaron had treated his sister, and he wasn't pleased."

Every muscle in Emily's body was tensed, something she'd regret later when she was sore. She was now leaning on the counter and waiting for the rest of the story, surprised at herself for being so caught up in this. "So he killed him?" she pressed. "Calvin tricked Aaron into eating peanuts?"

A small smile spread across Alyssa's face at Emily's enthusiasm. "Calvin easily admitted to being unhappy about Calvin and Zoe's relationship. He was very calm and cool when I first started talking to him. I think his conscience finally got to him, though. He admitted that he slipped some peanut oil into Aaron's food just before his break. Calvin never intended for Aaron to die. He just wanted him to feel bad for a while and to get a bit of revenge. Calvin had never seen Aaron actually have a reaction to any of the foods in the restaurant, and he'd even seen him serve a dish with peanut sauce to someone before. He thought at the very worst it'd give Aaron a stomachache, and it would look like a simple accident. Actually seeing him dead in the alley, however, was an entirely different matter."

"That it was," Emily agreed. "Calvin had even been the one to bring me a glass of water when he found out what happened. I guess I'm just lucky I wasn't allergic to anything."

"I genuinely don't think he would've done anything like that," Alyssa said quietly as she buried her fingers in Rosemary's fur. "It's interesting, you know. When I first joined the police force, my parents were very worried that I'd see some horrible things and be scarred for life. And I *have* seen some horrible things, but I've also seen a lot of people who just made really bad mistakes. Calvin will end up serving time for what he's done, but I highly doubt this is something he'll do again."

Emily studied her new friend closely. She was young, younger than Emily's own children. She still had so much life ahead of her and so much to learn, and yet she was quite astute. "You're very good at your job, aren't you?"

A blush of pink crept over Alyssa's cheeks. "I'm passionate about it, anyway. I want to be chief inspector someday, but I've still got a long way to go."

"I imagine your breakthrough in this case will only help that," Emily noted.

Alyssa tipped her head to the side uncertainly. "I guess so, but I feel bad about it. I don't think I'd ever have had this sort of break in the investigation if it weren't for you. On the other hand, I don't think Chief Inspector Woods would've listened to me if I'd gone ahead and put it all together for him the way you did for me. He was fine with hearing that you'd remembered a few things, but beyond that…" She gave a helpless shrug.

Emily reached across the counter and patted her hand. "Don't worry about any of that, dear. I'm just glad that the case was solved, and you might as well get a boost to your career. I'm also starting to get used to the fact that folks don't pay attention to older people like me. It's something I just need to learn to accept. I might even make a fantastic spy if it weren't for this red hair!" she laughed.

Checking her watch, Alyssa hopped down from the stool. "I'd better get going. My shift starts soon. Woods doesn't even know I'm here talking to you about this, and he probably wouldn't be too pleased if he did. It's completely against protocol to release information like this to anyone but the families, but considering how involved you were, I thought it only fitting."

"Your secret is perfectly safe with me, as long as you promise not to tell anyone what a mess my place was today!" Emily laughed again as she escorted Alyssa to the front door. She was feeling particularly light-hearted in knowing that the truth about Aaron's death had been revealed. It didn't change the fact that he was dead, of course, and there were probably all sorts of things that his family and friends would still need to take care of, but it was good to know that at least the problem of what exactly had happened was resolved.

"It's completely fine," Alyssa reassured her again. "I'm sorry. I meant to ask how your blog was going."

Emily lifted her shoulders and let them fall. "Considering the way this house smells right now, I don't think you'll be seeing me featured on any morning talk shows anytime soon!"

"I'm sure I'll see you around. Bye. Bye, Rosemary." With one last pet on the cat's head, Alyssa was heading out to her car.

"Goodbye!" Emily closed the door behind her and went back into the kitchen. The motivation to cook she'd felt earlier in the day had been drained by the burned casserole. Even the knowledge of Aaron's true cause of death was starting to make her realize just how tired she was. "I think I was just keeping myself busy so I wouldn't think about it," she told the cat. "Let's try this casserole, shall we?"

Getting out a plate, Emily dished up a small portion. It looked good enough, despite the burned edge, and she sank her fork into the creamy concoction. She put it in her mouth and spit it right back out again. "Oh, that's terrible! I think I forgot something. Here. Why don't you try it?"

Emily set the plate on the floor for the cat. She fetched a glass and some water so she could get the taste out of her mouth. By the time she turned around, Rosemary had completely polished it off.

"At least it's not a complete waste."

CHAPTER NINE

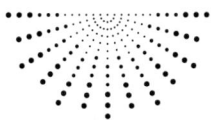

"It smells amazing in here, Mom!" Phoebe gasped as she came in through the front door two nights later.

"Is it yucky stuff?" Ella asked, holding her teddy bear under one arm.

"Ella! We talked about that!"

Emily, of course, wasn't offended in the slightest. "I don't think it's yucky stuff. It did turn out yucky when I made it the other day, but it's much better this time."

Her granddaughter swung her bear around to her front so she was holding it in front of her stomach, almost protectively. "Are you sure?"

"I'm quite sure, but you'll just have to taste them for yourself. Hello, Mavis. Nathan and Genevieve, so glad you could come." Emily stood, happy to play hostess as the rest of her family arrived.

Nathan kissed her on the cheek. "I was surprised when you said you wanted to cook for all of us. That's a lot. Are you sure there isn't anything we can do? It wouldn't take a moment to pop down to the store and grab something."

Emily waved him toward the dining room. "Don't even think about it. I've got it all taken care of and waiting for you. I've just promised Ella here that it isn't even yucky this time, so you'll all have to tell me if I'm right or not."

A few minutes later, everyone was seated. Emily had cooked up another—much bigger—

batch of the Venetian soup, which had been rather delicious the first round. She'd also redone the casserole, and a quick sample in the kitchen had told her it was fit to serve this time. With some vegetables and bread, it made a complete meal. She watched eagerly as everyone dug in.

"I didn't think I liked seafood," Matthew said quietly when he was nearly done with his first bowl of soup and eyeing the tureen for another one. He glanced at his wife. "You'll have to get the recipe for this one, love."

Phoebe nodded enthusiastically. "Did you try the other one yet? Mom, this is fantastic!"

Ella bobbed her head in agreement. "You were right! It's not yucky!"

Lucy straightened her shoulders and tossed back her head, trying to look important and ladylike. "It's very delicious, Gran."

Genevieve dabbed a bit of broth from her mouth. "It's incredible!"

"Thank you." Emily watched with great satisfaction as they all got their fill. To see that even the girls, who might be a little more picky given their young ages, enjoyed their meal was the best reward for all her hard work she ever could've gotten.

When the forks and spoons slowed down and everyone was starting to get full, Emily knew the conversation was about to start up again. "Lucy, Ella, I have a surprise waiting for you in the upstairs bedroom. Why don't you head up there?"

"Really?" Lucy was already out of her chair.

Ella was close behind. "What is it?"

"You'll have to go and see!" Emily replied.

"Be careful on the stairs," Phoebe called after them. She turned to her mother. "It's not a bunch of candy, is it?"

"Not at all," Emily assured her. "Just a little something I picked up while Anita and I were out shopping. Did you all truly like the meal?"

"It was remarkable," Mavis said, still staring at her empty plate. "Is this all because of your blog? For some reason, I thought you were going to do restaurant reviews."

Emily nodded. She'd known all of this would need to come about eventually, and this seemed the best way to do it. "It started out that way, yes," she admitted. "Unfortunately, I was at The Silver Swan on the day that young waiter was found dead."

"What?" Nathan exploded. "And you didn't tell me? Are you all right?"

Genevieve looked pale, and Mavis put her hand over her mouth. Phoebe's arm moved slightly, and Emily thought she was probably reaching for Matthew's hand under the table.

Emily smiled. These people gathered here at the table were constantly worrying about her. This was exactly the reaction she'd expected from them, but now she was a little more prepared for it. They meant well, and even if they treated her like she was older and more frail than she was, it was only because they cared. "I'm perfectly fine. It's actually quite a tale."

Genevieve circled her hand in the air, making her rings sparkle. "I think we're all very interested in hearing it!"

Emily explained to them how she'd waited too long for her food and witnessed Aaron fighting with the chef. To make it a more exciting story, she went ahead and explained that she'd already seen the young man in an argument with his girlfriend as well, even if she hadn't quite put those pieces together at the time. Seeing her children's faces riveted to hers, she continued. The grocery store, the funeral, all of it.

"It was the seafood itself and Toby's allergy to it that made me think a bit harder about Aaron, you see," she explained. "That and finding out that Aaron worked with his girlfriend's brother. There's a very smart detective constable who was willing to listen to what I had to say, and she really deserves the credit for putting it all together.

"Well," Nathan said, putting his napkin down, "I think I'll have to call the chief inspector and give him an earful. He should've contacted me right away. Finding a dead body isn't the kind of thing a woman of your age can recover from easily."

"You'll do no such thing," Emily asserted, waving her finger in the air. "If anything, Chief Inspector Woods did too much to try to take care of me. He was quite concerned over me, had a paramedic look me over, and even offered me a ride home. The thing is, Nathan, I'm an adult. I may be older than you, but that only means that I have more experience. I might not know everything about marketing or computers, but I'm quite capable of taking care of myself. If I needed a ride, then I'd have called."

Her poor son looked flabbergasted, but Emily was proud. She'd finally told him exactly how she felt. It didn't have to be mean or assertive, but it did get the job done.

"I have to say, all of this is very unexpected," Mavis said in wonderment. "You've had quite an adventure this week. I can see why you didn't want to do more restaurant reviews, but it's obvious we were wrong about the rest of it. Maybe you really should be a food blogger."

"I think the restaurants would be a possibility again, except that I'm not sure I'm going to stick with food, after all," Emily admitted.

"You're not going to do the blog?" Phoebe looked disappointed.

"I am," Emily corrected. "I'm just not sure that food is quite the right niche for me. I'm still going to bake cookies with the girls, of course. I promised them that, and you know I won't go back on it. But eating out at restaurants or buying all sorts of expensive ingredients adds up to quite a lot. Most of the time, Rosemary and I don't really need that much food around the house. I think I might find something else to do."

Nathan cleared his throat. Apparently he'd gotten over his shock at her involvement in the murder case, because he had that serious look on his face again that told Emily he was about to tell her what to do. "I know you want to find something that entertains you, Mother, but I'd seriously advise against jumping topics. Your followers have already come to expect articles about food. You've got the restaurant review and two recipes under your belt—or at least, I'm assuming you'll be writing about all that—and if you switch it up now you might upset them. If they've come to your website expecting recipes and they find something completely different, you'll probably lose some of your audience.

Emily smiled at her son. Again, she knew he meant well. He only wanted to see her succeed. That was the thing with Nathan, though. He was always about success. He just didn't understand that some things were worth doing simply on their own merit, whether money was involved or not. Blogging was supposed to be fun, and she was determined to keep it that way. "I don't think they'll mind, considering it's just the five of you and Anita!"

"So what are you going to write about instead?" Phoebe asked.

"I think she's going to become a private investigator," Mavis said with a grin. "You only have to take a few courses, and you'd be all set to go. Everyone thinks of them as some guy in a trench coat, but nobody would suspect you. Then you could write about that!"

Emily had to laugh. "I don't think that's quite up my alley! I'm not sure what I want to do just yet, but I'll find something. I've already worked up the first few blog posts, and it was a lot of fun. More fun than even I expected it to be. Of course, next time it probably won't be nearly as eventful."

Nathan was scratching his chin. "You could do a blog about retirement. There are probably quite a few people your age who would love to read about someone else's experience with pensions and budgeting."

"And dealing with annoying adult children who constantly think they know better?" Phoebe joked.

"Now, now." Emily shook her head. "I thought food was a great idea because it brings people together. It's certainly given me a conversation starter or two. I'll figure out what I want to focus on next, and that's when I'll worry about it. I have all the time in the world, so I'm not worried about it."

"Well, then." Nathan lifted his glass. "A toast to the new blog, whatever it may be about!"

"Here, here!" They all raised their glasses, clinking them and laughing happily.

Emily knew she was the happiest, because she had her family around her.

"Gran! Gran!"

The girls came galloping down the stairs, their arms full of toys. Rosemary came trotting down after them.

"Do be careful!" Phoebe reminded them.

"Look at this!" Ella dumped a handful of toy pots and pans into her mother's lap.

"Daddy! Can I make you some soup?" Lucy asked, holding up a little metal pot with a small wooden spoon stuck in the top of it. "It's a new recipe I found."

"That would be lovely, sweetheart." Matthew gestured toward his empty bowl. "You can put it right in there for me."

"How darling." Phoebe picked up some of the little dishes. "Is this what you got them?"

"I was a little inspired," Emily admitted. "I always loved playing with this kind of thing when I was a little girl, and so did you. We all have to eat sometime, so we might as well enjoy it."

"Mm mm!" Matthew enthused as his eldest daughter stood by. "Best soup I've ever had. Just don't tell Gran!"

Emily smiled. She might not be blogging about food any longer, but it really did have a way of bringing people together.

THANK YOU FOR CHOOSING A PUREREAD BOOK!

We hope you enjoyed the story, and as a way to thank you for choosing PureRead we'd like to send you this free Special Edition Cozy, and other fun reader rewards…

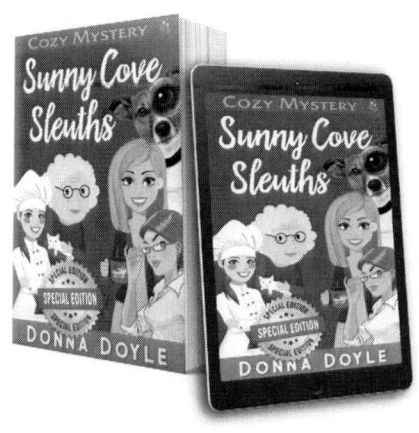

Click Here to download your free Cozy Mystery PureRead.com/cozy

Thanks again for reading.
See you soon!

EMILY'S NEXT ADVENTURE...

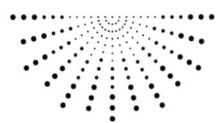

A CRAFTY CASE OF MURDER AT THE FAIR

Grandma Emily, the unwitting amateur sleuth, stumbles into another troubling crime at the craft fair...

"Look what I made, Gran!"

"Oh, how delightful. Tell me all about it." Emily Cherry studied the ball of red clay that her youngest granddaughter held in the air. It didn't look like much to her, but she understood that beauty was often in the eyes of the beholder.

"Well, it's a ladybug!" Ella replied sweetly.

"And it's quite a beautiful one," Emily replied. "What about you, Lucy? What are you making?"

At six years old, Lucy had elaborated slightly on her creation. She had her tongue peeking out of the corner of her mouth as she carefully added darker blue pieces to the side of the light blue blob on the table. "It's a bluebird!"

"How very nice, and both of your sculptures are wonderful. What do you think you might do with them?" Emily herself was carefully crafting a small flower in the palm of her hand, pressing the end of a toothpick into each petal to create some texture. It was so nice to spend time with her grandchildren and just forget about all the troubles of the world while she focused only on being creative.

"I'm going to give mine to Mommy," Ella said proudly as she searched the table for some black clay to add to her ladybug. "Do you think she'll like it?"

"Of course she will," Emily reassured her.

"I bet she'll put them up on the shelf in the kitchen where she can see them every day," Lucy added.

Pride swelled in Emily's chest to hear this. Lucy and Ella, just like any pair of sisters, didn't always get along well. It was good to see Lucy building up her little sister that way. "That sounds like a very nice place for your sculptures. I'm sure your Mommy would be happy to do that."

"Right now, she's happy to be at her book club," Lucy replied. "Every evening she sits down to read her book, and she has a little pad on the end tables where she takes notes so she can remember what to talk about with her friends."

"I miss her, though," Ella said as she poked big blobs of black clay onto her little statue. "I like it when Mommy is home."

"Your Mommy likes to be at home with you, too," Emily reminded her gently, setting down her clay tools to rub her hand gently down Ella's back. The poor little thing was only three, and she was used to having her mother at home all the time. "That's why she's always here with you. But she needs time to do things for herself as well. And she'll be home soon. Then your Daddy will be home as well. For right now, we can enjoy our time together, right?"

Ella's big brown eyes looked worried as she thought about it, but then they brightened. She wrapped her arms around Emily's middle. "Yeah."

"That's a dear." It was a dreary, rainy day, and Emily had worried about whether or not she and the girls would find anything fun to do. Going outside to play simply wasn't an option unless she wanted them to be completely soaked to the bones. Fortunately, she had plenty of craft supplies on hand, and the girls had happily dived in.

"Gran, what's that thing you're writing? On the computer?" Ella asked.

"My blog?" Emily asked. "I haven't done much of anything with that for a while." She'd been very excited about the prospect when she'd first made the decision to start writing. Being a retired widow had meant that she needed something to fill her time, and the blog had felt like the perfect outlet. Unfortunately, the discovery of a murder victim and the drama that'd ensued afterward had made her feel a little less enthusiastic. It didn't help that she hadn't had any more followers than her best friend and her family members.

"Yeah, that! You should do your crafts on there."

Lucy cast a sidelong glance at her sister. "She puts food on her blog, not crafts."

"Well, that's what I *was* doing," Emily corrected gently. There were a few times when she'd pulled out a new recipe or made a nice pie and had considered taking a few photos and making a post, but she hadn't quite been able to make herself do it. "I was thinking about doing something completely different with it."

"Crafts would be fun, then," Lucy replied. "And we could help you!"

And the more they created, as several little creatures and flowers and other random sculptures that couldn't be identified accumulated on the kitchen table, Emily was starting to like the idea more and more. "Let's get a few photos of these. I think I'll take your advice. My very first craft post can be all about my rainy-day crafts that I did with my granddaughters. How about that?"

The girls cheered their approval as Emily picked up her cell phone and turned on the camera. She snapped pictures of each little item, making sure to include the girls in some of the photos as well. They gleefully smiled and giggled and gave her ideas about what she could write.

"You could tell them how to make a ladybug," Ella suggested.

"Or a bluebird," Lucy added. "And you could show all the different parts of your flower and then how to put them together. I've seen some videos like that."

"Have you?" Emily raised an eyebrow. She'd started watching a lot more videos online as she was working to start up her blog, and she'd quickly discovered that you could learn just about anything with the information that was available on the internet. "Perhaps I'll have to look into some of those."

"I have some drawing videos that I like to watch. I can show you sometime."

"Let's do that. Oh, Rosemary!" Emily exclaimed as her fluffy cat jumped up on the table and pressed her face into a lump of clay.

Lucy clapped her hands. "Take a picture of her!"

"You think she should be a part of this, too?" Emily laughed.

"Yes!" Ella agreed.

Rosemary cooperated perfectly, nosing something here or batting gently at a ball of clay. Her wild, crooked whiskers quivered as she sniffed and played, even though she was making more of a mess than they already had made.

Phoebe walked in to find her mother and daughters laughing and giggling around the table just after Rosemary had jumped back down. "It looks like you guys are having a great time."

"Did you like your book party?" Ella asked, having completely forgotten about how lonely she was now that they were having a raucous good time.

"Book club," Phoebe reminded her. "And we had a wonderful time. I even got to help pick out the next book that we're going to read. We'll have to take a trip to the library later this week to get a copy. You girls can get some books, too."

"We need books about crafting!" Lucy urged. "Gran is going to make her blog all about crafts, and we're going to help!"

"Is that so?" Phoebe looked at Emily.

"Yes!" Ella added before Emily had a chance to explain. "And Rosemary is going to help, too! She's in a lot of our pictures!"

Emily gestured toward the stairs. "Why don't you girls go up to the spare bedroom and make sure you've picked up all the toys you were playing with earlier. We don't want to leave that a mess."

"Okay, Gran!" The girls stomped up the stairs.

Emily watched them go, almost regretting that it was time for them to leave. "We've had a very good afternoon," she told her daughter. "I do wonder how you'd feel about the idea of the craft blog, though."

Phoebe lifted a shoulder. "It's not really up to me what you do with it, Mom."

"No, but I'd really like to keep the girls involved as much as I can. I wanted to check with you and see if it'd be all right to put some of their pictures on the website." Emily pulled up the photos she'd just snapped and turned the screen around to show her daughter.

"Oh, how precious," Phoebe cooed as she flipped through them. "If that's what you want to do, then it's fine with me."

"I'm glad. The girls have gotten me inspired all over again. I was honestly starting to think I wasn't going to do anything with my blog anymore. Things had gotten a little nutty when it came to the food blog, and I had considered a few options for a different topic. None of them had really appealed, but the girls' enthusiasm has gotten the old creative juices going again."

"Good for you! Now, just don't say anything to Nathan. You know he'll have something to say about it." Phoebe rolled her eyes about her older brother.

Nathan was a marketing consultant, and he always had advice ready to go. It didn't matter if anyone wanted it or not. Emily laughed. "He'll deal with it. I'm sure he'll tell me that craft blogs don't appeal to anyone but other crafters, but I really don't mind. I'm not doing this with the idea of making a bunch of money or gathering as many followers as I can. I just need a creative outlet every now and then, and I think it's about time that I started it up again."

"Good for you," Phoebe said enthusiastically. "I don't have a lot of friends who craft, but they'll probably be happy to see the girls. When you get some posts up, I'll send the link out and maybe get you some new followers."

"You can do that if you'd like, but don't feel like you have to. I don't want any of this to be a burden on anyone else."

"Don't be silly, Mom. You're never a burden. Girls, are you ready to go? I've got to get dinner started!"

Lucy and Ella came rushing back down the stairs. "Can we get hamburgers?" Lucy asked.

"Yeah!" Ella agreed.

"I already have some chicken thawed out, so maybe another time. Be sure and thank your Gran for spending time with you."

The girls barreled into Emily, wrapping their little arms around her and assuring her that they couldn't wait to see her again and help her get started on her blog. Phoebe thanked her as well, and then the next thing Emily knew, the house was eerily silent again.

She walked into the kitchen and began putting the finished sculptures on a tray so they could dry. "You know, Rosemary, I think we've got a lot of work ahead of us. I'll have to get into the craft bins and see what else I have. I'm sure I have some yarn. It's been a while since I've picked up a crochet hook, but it could be an interesting post as I try to figure out if I still know what I'm doing, right?"

Rosemary perked up her ears and followed Emily to the storage closet, sticking her face in the first bin Emily opened. She reached in carefully with her paw and patted at a bag of beads.

"Yes, jewelry wouldn't be a bad option. The girls would like that, too. I'll set that out for them. Oh, but I don't think I have any beading thread. I'll have to start a list for when I go to the hobby store." Emily got back up to grab a pad of paper. This was going to be fun, indeed…

Fun indeed? It certainly is for our readers when Emily stumbles into another crafty crime at the craft fair...

Inspired by her arty granddaughters to share her love of yarn, clay, and beads with the whole world, **the last thing Grandma Cherry expects is a mystery to unravel right before her eyes**!

Armed with her quick wit and sharp eye **the unassuming senior quickly crafts a plan to uncover the motive for murder** in what seems like a peaceful community.

Will she find the felon? Are they hiding in plain sight? And how will Emily Cherry dig deep enough the find the culprit among the crafts?

Continue Reading and find out on Amazon…

OTHER BOOKS IN THIS SERIES

If you loved this story and want to follow Emily's antics in other fun easy read mysteries continue **dive straight into other books in this series...**

Read them all...

A Troubling Case Of Murder On The Menu

A Crafty Case Of Murder At The Fair

A Hairy Case of Murder At The Animal Sanctuary

A Clean & Tidy Case of Murder - A Truly Messy Mystery

A Cranky Case of Murder at the Autostore

A Colorful Case of Stolen Art at the Gallery

A Frightful Case of Murder in the Fashion Store

A Beastly Case of Murder at the Bookstore

A Murky Case of Murder at the Movies

A Closing Case of Murder For Emily Cherry

SO MUCH MORE TO ENJOY!

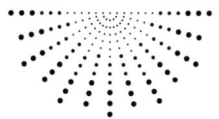

Along with Emily's adventures, you can also dive into these magnificent cozy mystery collections and boxsets…

All are free to read on Kindle Unlimited

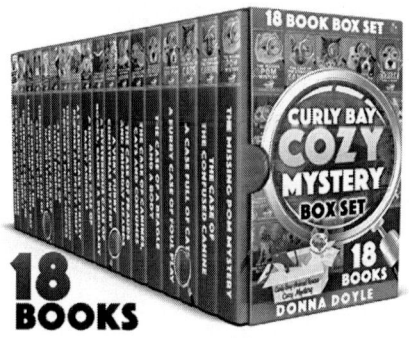

Read The Curly Bay Box Set

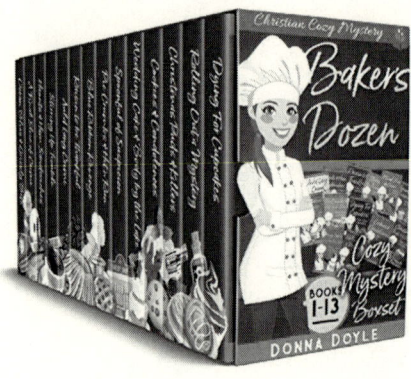

Read the Baker's Dozen Boxset

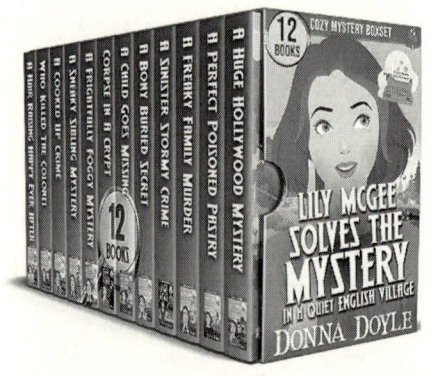

Read the Lily McGee Boxset

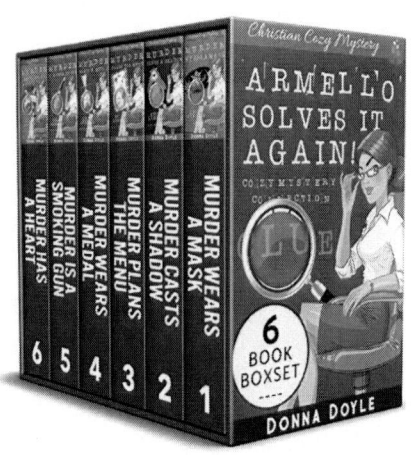

Read the Kelly Armello Boxset

OUR GIFT TO YOU

AS A WAY TO SAY THANK YOU WE WOULD LOVE TO SEND YOU THIS SPECIAL EDITION COZY MYSTERY FREE OF CHARGE.

Our Reader List is 100% FREE

Click Here to download your free Cozy Mystery **PureRead.com/cozy**

At PureRead we publish books you can trust. Great tales without smut or swearing, but with all of the mystery and romance you expect from a great story.

Be the first to know when we release new books, take part in our fun competitions, and get surprise free books in your inbox by signing up to our Reader list.

As a thank you you'll receive this exclusive Special Edition Cozy available only to our subscribers...

Click Here to download your free Cozy Mystery **PureRead.com/cozy**

Thanks again for reading.
See you soon!

Made in United States
North Haven, CT
13 January 2025

64378742R00095